Dragon
Mountain

DRAGON
MOUNTAIN

Tim Vyner

Collins

An Imprint of HarperCollinsPublishers

First published in Great Britain by HarperCollins Publishers Ltd in 1996
10 9 8 7 6 5 4 3 2 1
First published in Picture Lions in 1997
10 9 8 7 6 5 4 3 2 1
Picture Lions is an imprint of the Children's Division, part of HarperCollins
Publishers Limited, 77-85 Fulham Palace Road, Hammersmith, London W6 8JB
Copyright © Tim Vyner 1996
A CIP catalogue record for this title is available from the British Library.
The author and illustrator assert the moral right to be identified as the
author and illustrator of the work.
ISBN: 0 00 198186-2 (hardback)
0 00 664585-2 (Picture Lions)
Printed and bound in Hong Kong

A huge, mysterious mountain overshadowed the tiny
house where Chin lived with his mother and father.
The mountain reached up so high into the swirling clouds
that Chin had never seen the top of it.

His father often told him stories of the mountain but the
one Chin loved most was about an old man and a dragon.

One day, Chin's father asked him to take their water
buffalo to sell at the market. It was a long walk and,
after a while, Chin stopped to let the buffalo drink.
As he sat gazing up at the mountain, he saw a narrow
path winding all the way up into the clouds.

Chin thought of his father's story. "He's the oldest man in the world, and he keeps a dragon who can blow the rain out of the clouds and breath fire to dry the land."

Chin tried to imagine what the dragon looked like; he thought it sounded the most wonderful creature that ever lived.

The mountain path looked so inviting.

"Surely it won't take very long to climb up and see the dragon for myself," thought Chin. And he tied up the water buffalo and set off. Up and up Chin climbed and, as he climbed higher, the stony path turned into steps cut deep into the mountainside.

At last Chin reached the top. There, in front of him, was an old, old man. He was bent and walked slowly with a stick. But if this was the man in his father's story, where was the dragon? The only creature in sight was a golden monkey.

"Hello," called Chin, "are you the old man with the dragon?" The old man shook his head.

"What dragon? I've lived many, many years but I have never seen a dragon," the old man said. Then, throwing his stick aside, he suddenly sprang to life.

"But I have seen the most beautiful creatures on this earth. I've seen a golden bird flying overhead with fire burning in its wings... a four-legged creature as big as a deer swimming deep in the water... and a huge furry creature with black eyes as big as bowls... I've seen cows with hair so long that it sweeps the dust from the ground... and thousands of tiny insects lighting up the night."

"Please tell me more," cried Chin, but the old man leant quietly on his stick. It suddenly seemed very still and silent at the top of the mountain and when Chin looked around for the steps all he could see were the clouds. He realised he must have been away for a very long time.

"Could you show me the way down?" he asked
the old man. Without a word, the old man and the
monkey led Chin to the top of the stairway before
vanishing into the mist again.

Chin soon found himself surrounded by a group
of tall trees.

Suddenly a ball of fire flashed by in the branches.

"It must be the dragon's fire," thought Chin, and
he hid away in the trees.

When Chin dared to peep up into the branches, it wasn't a dragon he saw but the most beautiful bird; a golden pheasant with wings so bright they glowed like burning flames. He remembered the old man's description of the bird with fire in its wings.

Chin carried on down the mountain until he came to a
stream. The water was so cool and fresh that Chin bent
down to take a drink.

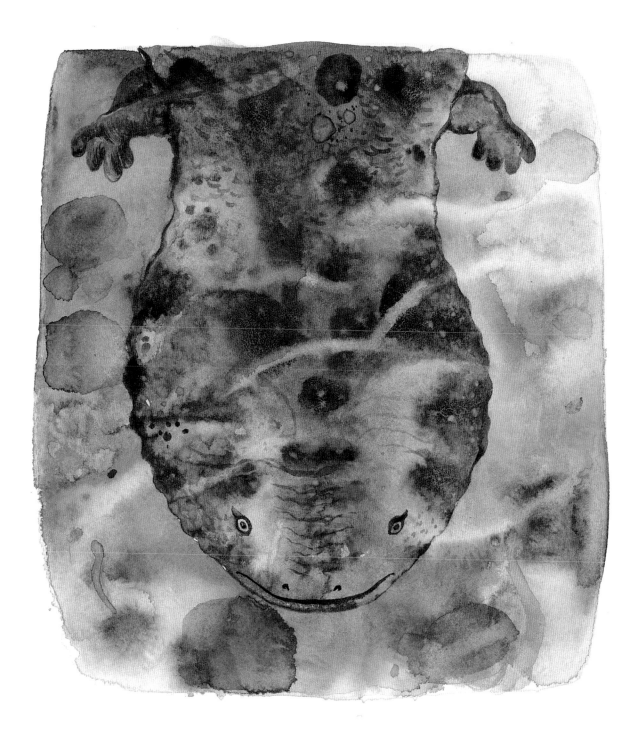

From the stream, a pair of mysterious eyes peered back at Chin and he wondered if this could be the dragon, hiding in the water.

The creature was very large and long, with four legs.
It was a giant salamander and not the dragon after all.

Once again, the old man's words came back to Chin and
he remembered the description of the water creature as
big as a deer.

Chin carried on until he came to a bamboo thicket.
By now he felt tired and he sat down for a moment's
rest. Soon Chin had fallen asleep.

His dreams were filled with dragons as big as
mountains, salamanders the size of houses, and
huge black eyes, shining in the dark...

Chin woke up with a start, and there before him
was a huge furry creature with the beautiful black
eyes that he had seen in his dream.

It was a giant panda just as the old man had described. Chin tried to have a closer look but the panda quickly hurried away.

By now the light was fading fast and Chin hurried on
feeling frightened and alone.

Suddenly he came to a clearing where the air
was filled with flashes of brightly coloured lights.
In the distance Chin could see the shape of a large creature
with long hair reaching to the ground, and he wondered
whether he had found the dragon at last.

But as his eyes grew used to the light, he saw that
the beast was really a yak and that the air was filled
with fire flies.

Once again, they were just how the old man had
described them. But still Chin had not seen the dragon.

Chin ran on until finally he reached the bottom of the mountain and found his water buffalo tied up near the river where he had left him. He hurried home along the familiar path. His father was waiting for him.

"Where have you been all day?" he shouted angrily.
"And why haven't you sold the buffalo?"

Chin told his father about the old man and all the
wonderful animals he had seen on the mountain.

"But Father, I didn't see the dragon. Does he really
live there?"

"No Chin, dragons only exist in stories! Now go to bed."

Chin felt so sad as he stood alone and gazed up at the mountain.

"I still believe in the dragon," thought Chin, "and even though the creatures I saw today were just as wonderful, I still want to see the dragon."

He stared at the mountain for a long time. Suddenly, as he looked, he thought he could make out a shape.

"The dragon!" he whispered. And there in the moonlight Chin saw his dragon, dancing as it curled around its mountain home.